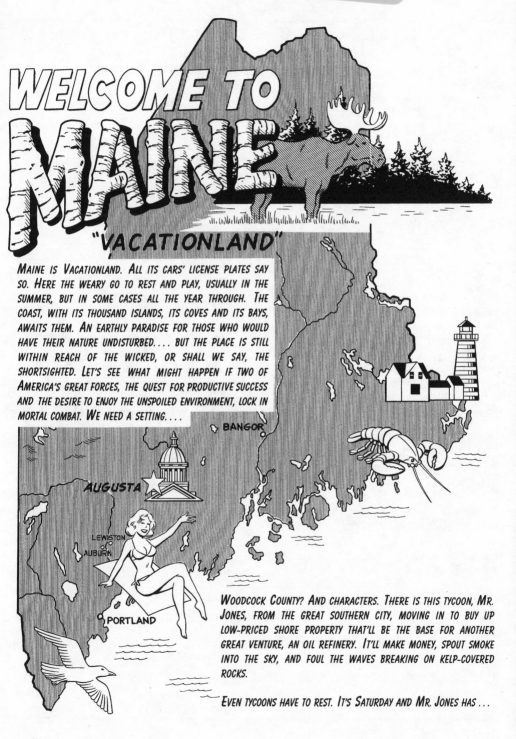

WELCOME TO MAINE

"VACATIONLAND"

MAINE IS VACATIONLAND. ALL ITS CARS' LICENSE PLATES SAY SO. HERE THE WEARY GO TO REST AND PLAY, USUALLY IN THE SUMMER, BUT IN SOME CASES ALL THE YEAR THROUGH. THE COAST, WITH ITS THOUSAND ISLANDS, ITS COVES AND ITS BAYS, AWAITS THEM. AN EARTHLY PARADISE FOR THOSE WHO WOULD HAVE THEIR NATURE UNDISTURBED.... BUT THE PLACE IS STILL WITHIN REACH OF THE WICKED, OR SHALL WE SAY, THE SHORTSIGHTED. LET'S SEE WHAT MIGHT HAPPEN IF TWO OF AMERICA'S GREAT FORCES, THE QUEST FOR PRODUCTIVE SUCCESS AND THE DESIRE TO ENJOY THE UNSPOILED ENVIRONMENT, LOCK IN MORTAL COMBAT. WE NEED A SETTING....

BANGOR

AUGUSTA

LEWISTON
AUBURN

PORTLAND

WOODCOCK COUNTY? AND CHARACTERS. THERE IS THIS TYCOON, MR. JONES, FROM THE GREAT SOUTHERN CITY, MOVING IN TO BUY UP LOW-PRICED SHORE PROPERTY THAT'LL BE THE BASE FOR ANOTHER GREAT VENTURE, AN OIL REFINERY. IT'LL MAKE MONEY, SPOUT SMOKE INTO THE SKY, AND FOUL THE WAVES BREAKING ON KELP-COVERED ROCKS.

EVEN TYCOONS HAVE TO REST. IT'S SATURDAY AND MR. JONES HAS ...

... GONE FISHING.

MURDER BY REMOTE CONTROL

Janwillem van de Wetering

Designed and illustrated by Paul Kirchner

BALLANTINE BOOKS • NEW YORK

ALL RIGHTS RESERVED UNDER INTERNATIONAL AND PAN-AMERICAN COPYRIGHT CONVENTIONS. PUBLISHED IN THE UNITED STATES OF AMERICA BY BALLANTINE BOOKS, A DIVISION OF RANDOM HOUSE, INC., NEW YORK, AND SIMULTANEOUSLY IN CANADA BY RANDOM HOUSE OF CANADA LIMITED, TORONTO. FIRST PUBLISHED IN DUTCH IN 1984 BY W & L BOEKEN, AMSTERDAM. COPYRIGHT VOOR NEDERLANDSE TAALGEBIED © 1984 BY W & L BOEKEN, AMSTERDAM.

LIBRARY OF CONGRESS CATALOG CARD NUMBER: 86-91099

ISBN 0-345-33269-5

MANUFACTURED IN THE UNITED STATES OF AMERICA

COVER AND INTERIOR ART BY PAUL KIRCHNER
COVER DESIGN BY BILL TOTH
INTERIOR DESIGN BY PAUL KIRCHNER

AHH, A BITE...

ABOUT TIME, TOO!

6

7

9

"WHO?" MR. JONES ASKED, WHEN HE COULD STILL ASK. GOOD QUESTION. IT COULD HAVE BEEN ANYBODY, HIDDEN ON THE SHORE. WHAT'S ON THE SHORE? FOUR HOUSES, OVER-LOOKING THE BAY. WHO LIVES IN THESE HOMES? WOULDN'T THE OWNERS BE PRIME SUSPECTS?

THERE'S MR. KANE, IN THE OLD CAPE FARMHOUSE. MR. KANE IS A MAINER, BORN AND BRED; HIS FOREFATHER FOUGHT THE INDIANS SO THAT HE COULD SETTLE THIS VERY COVE.

JOHN DEERE

THE PRESENT MR. KANE IS A SELF-SUFFICIENT OLD MAN, LIVING OFF HIS FARM, A SMALL HOLDING NOW, SINCE MOST OF THE SHORE HAS BEEN SOLD OFF. KEPT COMPANY BY HIS ANIMALS AND MACHINES, HE FEELS NO NEED TO SOCIALIZE, BUT HE KNOWS HIS NEIGHBORS AND KEEPS AN EYE ON WHAT GOES ON. HE HAS OBSERVED MR. JONES AND KNEW OF HIS PLANS.

MAYBE MR. KANE DIDN'T LIKE MR. JONES.

11

A VICTORIAN MANSION PURCHASED BY VALERIE CURTIN, A STILL-YOUNG LADY FROM NEW YORK CITY, A WOMAN OF SOME MEANS WHO KEEPS TO HERSELF.

VALERIE LIKES GARDENING AND GROWS CAREFULLY CULTURED HERBS BETWEEN THE ROSES, MAGIC PLANTS THAT PROVIDED UNDERSTANDING DURING THE DREAMTIME THAT THE WHITE MAN DISTURBED. INSIGHT AND ENTERTAINMENT HIDE IN THE HERBS' LEAVES AND ROOTS AND ARE RELEASED WHEN VALERIE BOILS HER BREWS.

THOSE WHO HAVE HAD TEA AT HER HOUSE BECOME SILENTLY THOUGHTFUL WHEN ASKED ABOUT THEIR EXPERIENCES. SOME TOWNSPEOPLE CLAIM VALERIE IS A WITCH, AND SHE IS SOMETIMES TROUBLED BY YOUNG VANDALS WHO TRAMPLE HER GARDEN. SHE SMILES AT THEIR SILLINESS AND THEY TAKE TO THEIR HEELS.

WHEN VALERIE'S STRENGTH EBBS IT IS RESTORED BY THE OCEAN'S FLOW. SHE CHOSE HER SURROUNDINGS DELIBERATELY.

WASN'T MR. JONES GOING TO SPOIL HER VIEW?

MAYBE ALL MAINE RESIDENTS ARE ODD, BUT SOME APPEAR ODDER. JOE MCLOON IS A RETIRED REBEL. JOE GOT HIMSELF INTO A LITTLE ACCIDENT A WHILE BACK AND IS NOW PARALYZED FROM THE WAIST DOWN. REBELS ARE OFTEN PRACTICAL FOLK, ALTHOUGH THEIR IDEAS MAY RUN COUNTER TO THE NORM. HAVING LOST THE USE OF SOME OF HIS PARTS, HE CHANGED HIS LOVELIES INTO HELPFUL SERVANTS. FOLLOWING JOE'S INSTRUCTIONS, THEY REMODELED HIS HOUSE AND CONSTRUCTED A NEW VEHICLE. THE CONTRAPTION RIDES THE RAMPS OF JOE'S HOME AND ALLOWS HIM TO ROAM WHEREVER HE PLEASES. MORE INVENTIVE THAN EVER BEFORE AND UNCHANGED IN HIS VIOLENCE, JOE SHOULD BE ABLE TO PROTECT HIS PRIVATE DOMAIN. CRIPPLED BUT STILL FIGHTING-FIT, HE WOULD WANT TO IMPRESS HIS LADIES WHILE RISING ABOVE HIS PAIN.

PERHAPS JOE CONSIDERED MR. JONES A WORTHY FOE.

13

STEVE GOODRICH GOT A MILLION FROM HIS LAST STARRING ROLE TO TOP OFF A HEAP OF GOLD MINED FROM PREVIOUS MOVIES. THERE'S A TIME TO CALL IT A DAY, WHILE THE GOING IS STILL GOOD, AND STEVE PULLED BACK. HE FOUND A SANCTUARY THAT WAS THE MAXIMUM NUMBER OF AMERICAN MILES FROM HOLLYWOOD'S MADNESS. STEVE BROUGHT MAN FRIDAY, HIS TRUSTED CARE-TAKER, SECRETARY, SIDEKICK AND MAJORDOMO, ERIK VAN HEINEKEN.

ERIK IS THE HANDYMAN ABOUT THE MANSION, BUT HIS EVER-SERVILE PRESENCE MASKS HIS ABILITY TO SET THE STAGE AND DIRECT HIS MASTER'S PERFORMANCE. TOGETHER MASTER AND SERVANT PLAY THEIR HARMLESS GAME.

WOULD STEVE AND ERIK BE HARMLESS IF MR. JONES DISTURBED THEIR GAME?

14

HERE IS THE COUNTY SHERIFF, A LOYAL LAWMAKING CITIZEN EVER ALERT TO PROTECT HIS PROPERTY. PATROLLING THE SHORE, HE HAS FOUND A DRIFTING BOAT AND THE CORPSE IT CONTAINS. MR. JONES HAS BEEN KILLED BY PERSON OR PERSONS UNKNOWN. AS A MURDER INVESTIGATION IS THE STATE POLICE'S PRIVILEGE, THE SHERIFF HAS RADIOED THE CAPITAL FOR ASSISTANCE.

GOT HIS HEAD STOVE IN, DID HE?

YEAH, BUT BY WHAT?

COMING IN ON BAR HARBOR FLIGHT 750, 1100 HOURS, ONE STATE DETECTIVE... JIM BRADY FROM AUGUSTA...

SHIT, THIS IS MY TURF...WHO NEEDS THOSE ASSHOLES?

BAH, WE'LL LET THE MOTHERFUCKER WAIT AWHILE FOR STARTERS, HAR HAR HAR!

15

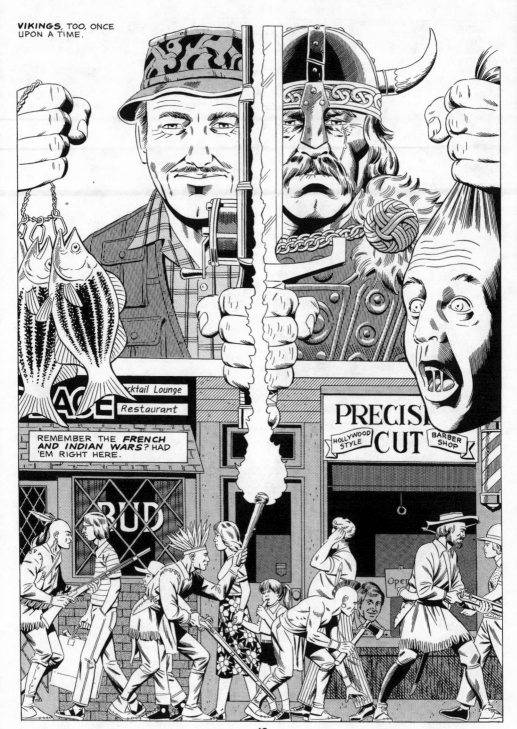

VIKINGS, TOO, ONCE UPON A TIME.

REMEMBER THE *FRENCH AND INDIAN WARS*? HAD 'EM RIGHT HERE.

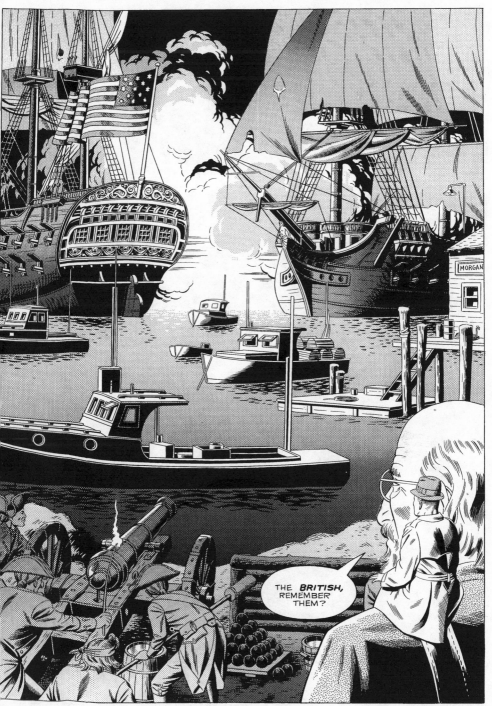

19

WE KNOW HIM... MAN BY THE NAME OF JONES... GUZZLES BEER WHILE HE FISHES... TOO MUCH THIS TIME... FELL OVER AND CRACKED HIS HEAD ON THE SIDE, COULD BE...

CALLED YOU IN ANYWAY... REGULATIONS, RIGHT?

WHERE'S THE EMPTY CANS?

THREW 'EM OVERBOARD.

THAT'S LITTERING. PITY HE CROAKED, COULD HAVE FINED HIM OTHERWISE.

WHAT'S WITH HIM?

ANYONE FLY TOY PLANES AROUND HERE?

NOW WHAT?

TOY PLANE.

WHAT OF IT?

23

A FEW MINUTES LATER...

24

25

26

GOT TO SIGN HERE... NORMALLY WE CUT THE GOVERNOR OUT, BUT SEEING YOU'RE A COP YOU'LL HAVE TO PAY THE SALES TAX TOO.

SO THEY GOT THE SON OF A GUN, DID THEY?

JONES? THEY SURE DID.

NEVER LIKED THAT JONES FELLOW. WANTED TO MUCK UP THE COAST, YOU KNOW...

OIL REFINERY INDEED... SEEMS WE ALREADY HAVE MORE SMOKE THAN WE RIGHTLY NEED.

AYUP... TURNED OUT TO BE A GOOD DAY AFTER ALL.

GRRRRR

BOW WOW WOW

ASSHOLE

27

SO YOUR NAME IS JIM, IS IT? MAY I CALL YOU THAT?

SURE.

I'M VALERIE. WHAT BRINGS YOU TO OUR COVE, JIM?

A LITTLE POLICE BUSINESS.

OH, HOW INTERESTING... SO YOU'RE A DETECTIVE?

YES.

HOW EXCITING.

GRRRR!

IT DOES HAVE ITS MOMENTS...

YIP!

YOU LIVE ALL ALONE HERE?

OH YES... I RETIRED ON MY SAVINGS.

31

YOU PLAY WITH MODEL AIRPLANES?

NO... I PREFER INDOOR SPORTS.

MR. JONES WAS KILLED WITH A MODEL AIRPLANE, RADIO-CONTROLLED.

THEY'RE SUCH NASTY AND NOISY LITTLE MACHINES. I'M SO GLAD WE DON'T HAVE THEM AROUND HERE.

YOU HAD ONE EARLIER ON THIS MORNING. YOU DIDN'T HEAR IT?

NO

AND YOU RIGHT OUT HERE, WORKING IN THE GARDEN...

36

37

38

YOU'RE A HANDY FELLOW, AREN'T YOU? GOT QUITE AN ARSENAL HERE.

EVER TRY TO MAKE A NICE LITTLE TOY PLANE?

POW

YOU STUPID DUMB PIGGY-BRAINED COP...

DO I HAVE TO SPELL IT OUT AGAIN?

EMILY IRONY SENT ME ON VACATION...

A LONG VACATION...

A VACATION FOR THE DURATION.

WHAT ELSE CAN I DO BUT PLAY GAMES? WITH MY PLAYMATES?

JUST PLAYFUL PRACTICE...

TO KEEP IN SHAPE...

TO STAY AWAKE.

40

42

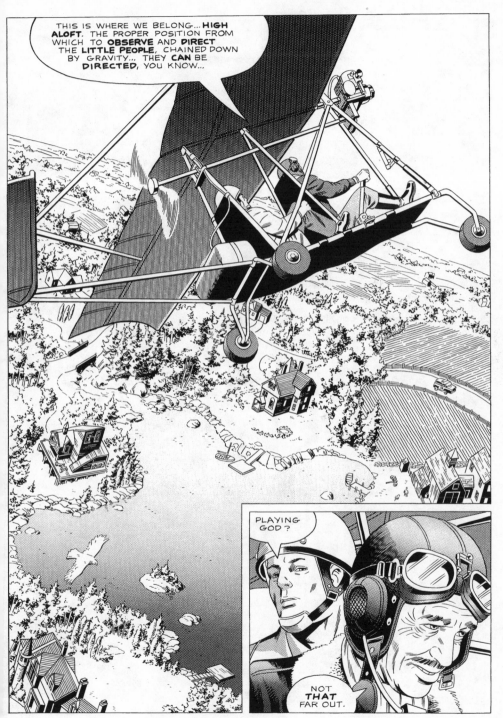

43

A LOT OF BIT PARTS GOING ON DOWN BELOW. BUT WHAT'S A SHOW WORTH IF NO ONE WATCHES?

HMMM

WHAT AM I MISSING?

POLICE

HARE KRISHNA UP IN THE SKY, FRESH SALAMI ON SEEDLESS RYE.

SHERIFF'S GOT SOME SUSPECT

POLICE

POLICE

45

WELL?

VERY NICE.. BUT WHERE I COME FROM THE SUN SEEMS TO SET IN THE WEST.

DOES IT NOW? I WOULDN'T KNOW...ERIK ALWAYS TAKES CARE OF THE SPECIAL EFFECTS...

VERY NICE OF YOU TO DROP BY. DO COME AGAIN.

OH YES. ALMOST FORGOT. ANY OR BOTH OF YOU HAPPEN TO KILL MR JONES?

GOODBYE!

BUT MY DEAR FELLOW, THE VERY IDEA!

ABER NEIN. FOR ZE RECORD I UMFUTTIKULLY STATE ZAT I KNOW NUZZING ABOUT NUZZING.

JUST ASKING. BYE NOW.

VOT A *BOZZERZUM* FELLOW!

RA*THER*!

46

47

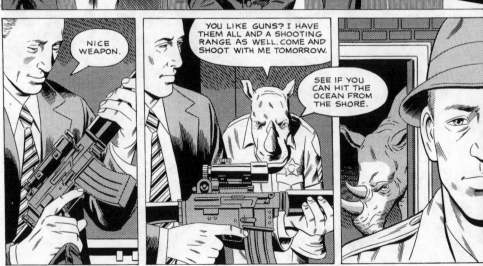

WHAT'S WRONG WITH THIS PUDDLE?

HEY!

NASTY LITTLE BASTARD, AREN'T YOU? WHAT'S YOUR NAME?

SOCIAL S. WELFARE III I LIVE IN THE STICKS.

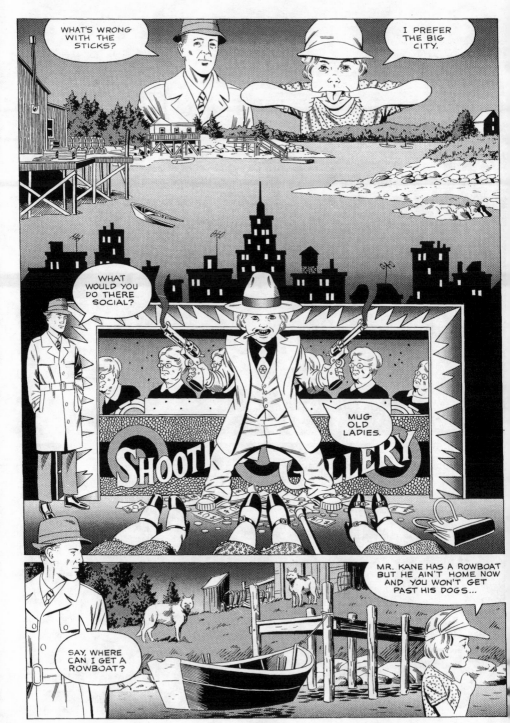

50

LIKE TO COME DOWN FOR A CUP OF TEA?

DON'T MIND IF I DO.

YOU WERE WITH OLD LOVERBOY ACROSS THE COVE?

SAW ME, DID YOU? AH, THIS *IS* THE LAND OF THE PURITANS, BUT WE ARE ALLOWED AFFAIRS I BELIEVE...

CAN'T KILL JONES, THOUGH

BUT I DIDN'T.

YOU *SURE* THIS IS TEA?

TEA FROM MY GARDEN. JONES WAS RATHER A NASTY MAN, YOU KNOW.

FUNNY TASTE.

MADE FROM A *FUNNY HERB*... YOU SEE, I WANT TO GET TO KNOW YOU BETTER, JIM.

I WANT TO SEE WHAT GOES ON IN THAT MIND OF YOURS... I PLAY A FAIR GAME... I DRANK THE TEA, TOO.

HERE WE GO...

IS THAT WHERE YOU'RE TAKING ME? THE CAPITAL'S CITY HALL?

I RECOGNIZE THE BUILDING... THAT MUST BE WHERE YOU WORK. DOES YOUR MIND ORIGINATE IN A MUSTY VAULT?

CITY HALL

THAT'S WHAT YOU'D LIKE ME TO BELIEVE... I WANT TO GET BEHIND THE FACADE.

AH, NOW WE'RE GETTING SOMEWHERE...

ARE WE? NO, YOU'RE *STILL* AVOIDING ME...

56

OH NO... BACK WHERE I STARTED.

ENOUGH OF THIS... I DETEST T.V.

WHAT'S IN THE TEA?

A TOUCH OF *PURE NATURE.*

PURE HEMLOCK AND NIGHTSHADE! KEEP YOURSELF TO YOURSELF, LADY!

DO YOU REALLY WANT ME TO DO THAT?

DO YOU?

LET'S TAKE ANOTHER TRIP... THIS TIME I'LL BE THE GUIDE.

COME ALONG...

THERE'S A GOOD DETECTIVE.

THE STARS ARE AWAITING US.

YOU'RE SO SWEET MY LOVE.

YOU MUST BE KIDDING

59

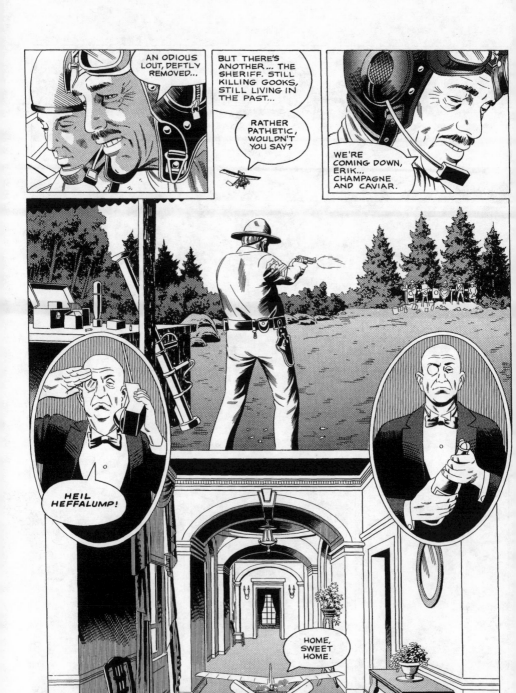

AN ODIOUS LOUT, DEFTLY REMOVED...

BUT THERE'S ANOTHER... THE SHERIFF. STILL KILLING GOOKS, STILL LIVING IN THE PAST...

RATHER PATHETIC, WOULDN'T YOU SAY?

WE'RE COMING DOWN, ERIK... CHAMPAGNE AND CAVIAR.

HEIL HEFFALUMP!

HOME, SWEET HOME.

THAT'LL HOLD THOSE LITTLE RICE-PROPELLED BASTARDS FOR NOW!

CONGRATULATIONS.

ISN'T IT TIME YOU GOT BACK? IF THAT NUT DIDN'T GET JONES THEN JONES JUST SMASHED HIS HEAD ON HIS DORY!

AND THE MODEL AIRPLANE?

FUCK THE MODEL AIRPLANE!

SHERIFF?

NOW WHAT?

THE SUSPECT IS GOING CRAZY.

SO? GET THE DOCTOR!

GOT HIM BUT HE WON'T DO NOTHING WITHOUT YOUR WRITTEN AUTHORITY.

SHIT! COMING, TEN-FOUR.

NOW FOR ACT TWO...

THIS THING SHOOTS?

GIMME THAT!

YOU SURE YOU WANT TO SHOOT UP YOUR VALUABLE PROPERTY THERE?

THEM *DUMB TREES?* WATCH THIS, *CHUMP!*

WAHOO!

BA-BOOM

WHA-?

64

STILL LOST IN THOUGHT, THE DETECTIVE DRIVES SLOWLY HOME TO HIS QUARTERS...

WHEN SUDDENLY...

WHAT'S THIS?

THEY'RE COMING STRAIGHT AT ME!

BETTER GET OFF THE ROAD...

70

SHERIFF SAYS HE DIDN'T GET JONES.

DON'T BELIEVE THE PIG, MAN. PUT THE SCREWS ON.

MAYBE *YOU* DID IT.

ME, KILL ANYONE?

LIFE IS A *SHORT SHIT*. THIS IS A FREE COUNTRY, I DON'T INTERFERE WITH OTHER PEOPLE'S CRAP.

MY GURU SAYS DIFFERENT.

ISN'T HE CUTE? LET'S HAVE HIM FOR DINNER!

73

75

THE NEXT MORNING...

MISSED ME?

SO?

DUNNO.

YOU GOT THE SHERIFF, THAT'S SOMETHING.

TOOK ME YEARS TO TRAIN THOSE KILLERS

YOU KILL JONES?

78

PLEASE STAY FOR LUNCH... I'LL FIX YOU SOMETHING GOOD. YOU LIKE LOBSTER?

REGULAR TEA?

DON'T WORRY, DEAR

YOU KILL JONES?

I'M A WOMAN... I GIVE LIFE.

SOME OF YOU HAVE BEEN KILLERS.

THERE'S NO BREAD IN THAT. I'M NICE...

NICE.

79

ONE, ADULT, TO SEE *STEVE GOODRICH.*

CERTAINLY, SIR. THREE DOLLARS, PLEASE.

PLEASE STEP RIGHT UP... THE SHOW BEGINS SHORTLY.

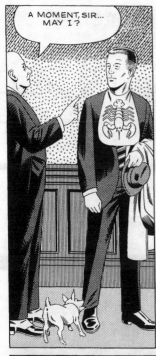

HOW SO, POIROT? EXPLAIN YOURSELF HOLMES. LET'S HAVE SOME LIGHT, MEUSSIEU MAIGRET.

THE OTHERS DIDN'T DO IT.

AND *WHY NOT*, PRAY?

YOU FORGOT THE QUESTION MARK.

IT ISN'T THERE.

FOR REASONS OF *SOUND COUNTRY THOUGHT, FEMINISM,* AND *OBSCURE THOUGH SELFISH PHILOSOPHY.*

DEDUCTION BY SUBTRACTION, AND I AM ALL YOU HAVE LEFT... BUT I MAY HAVE MY OWN DEFENSIVE REASONS...

WHY ME DUPIN?

WELL?

YOU TELL ME.

JA!

HERR HAUPTMANN, HOW SO?

ERIK VAN HEINEKEN WAS WITH THE **SS** BEFORE HE CHANGED HIS NAME AND HIS ALLEGIANCE.

WITH ZE DIVISION *GROSSDEUTSCHLAND*, RANK OF *OBERSTURM-BAHNFÜHRER!*

WOW.

KLIK

TELL HIM, HERR GENERAL -- HE CAN PROVE *NUZZING* ANYWAYS.

TELL A TALE?

JA!

89

91

A LITTLE SCHNAPS FOR THE FINAL JOURNEY, MEIN HERR?

ERIK, YOU ANTICIPATE MY VERY LAST WISH.

MY VERY LAST WISH...

I'M SCARED.

CUT! LET'S DO THIS RIGHT, STEVE. THIS IS YOUR FINEST ROLE... THE PART YOU WERE BORN TO PLAY!

THE CAMERA IS ROLLING, THE AUDIENCE IS WATCHING.

DIRECTOR

THE SWANSONG IS ALWAYS THE BEST PERFORMANCE. LET'S GO FOR THE OSCAR!

★EXTRA★
STEVE GOODRICH MAKES ULTIMATE SACRIFICE!

GIVES LIFE FOR FELLOW MAN!

MILLIONS MOURN!

ROGER!